FAST BREAK

A NICK O'FLANIGAN STORY

TROY LAMBERT

Fast Break

A Nick O'Flannigan Story

by Troy Lambert

Published by
CCMbooks
Boise, ID USA
www.capitalcitymurders.com

First Physical Release December 2022

 Created with Vellum

narrator, Joseph Stevenson and the team at Larson Sound Studios do a great job on them.

In the meantime, be well. Nick and I will see you as we travel the country together!

CONTENTS

But a sense of dread comes over him every time he thinks about it. His girlfriend even seems to have doubts.

With his parents, scouts and a huge crowd watching, Nick's life will change forever.

Find out where it all started in the Nick O'Flannigan story, *Fast Break*. Enjoy!

POINTS AND NUMBERS

Nick O'Flannigan stretched his legs out as far as they could go. His large feet bumped the desk in front of him.

"Watch it, O'Flannigan," the student in front of him hissed.

"Sorry," Nick mumbled.

This course in forensic accounting required a lot of his attention, but they certainly didn't make the desks in this classroom for a six-and-a-half-foot basketball player.

A senior at Boston College, Nick wanted an NBA career but had no illusions it would last forever. Thus his major in accounting. He could've joined the NBA early, but he wanted his degree, not only as a backup plan but something to do after he left the league.

His eye for detail helped him spot discrepancies in accounts, and his meticulous nature made him excel at solving problems and developing processes. That same skill fueled his only other hobby, photography, specifically macro photography. The more detailed the shot, the more Nick strived for the perfect angle.

He had an artistic side, but he leaned toward realism rather than abstract ideas. He wrote well and did well in English classes, something he knew would pay off in business later on.

A tiny ball of paper struck him in the cheek and fell toward his lap. Instinctively, he looked to see where it had come from. Smiling at him from a couple of rows over was Susie, one of the cheerleaders and a fellow senior.

Secondary education, not accounting, was her chosen major, but she had picked up this class in part out of interest in the subject, and partly because of Nick's presence.

She waved her fingers at him, then pointed to the paper in his hand.

He unfolded it and read the words there.

"See you tonight at 7." A drawn heart replaced the period.

Nick smiled up at her and nodded.

"Mr. O'Flannigan?" the professor asked from the front of the room. "Care to join us?"

Nick looked at him. "Certainly. Sorry about that." He sat up straighter and as he did, his knee smacked against the bottom of the desk.

"Ouch!" he grumbled. A titter of laughter came from the students around the room.

"Now that you're back, can you explain what's happening in this scenario?"

"Absolutely." Nick studied the problem on the board, one similar to an accounts receivable error in a test question recently. He'd gotten an "A" on that one and every other test in the class.

From his seat, he explained confidently what he saw.

"Good eye," the teacher replied. "Now, who can follow up with the approach we would take to resolve this issue and correct the profit and loss statement?"

Nick grinned and glanced over at Susie, but she was now paying rapt attention to the class and taking notes. These things did not come as easily to her as they did to him, and they'd initially met through a statistics study group a couple of years before.

Tonight would be an epic dinner date he hoped would impress her.

R ight after the accounting class ended, Nick shoved his books in his backpack and headed to the gym locker room. Before his date tonight he had basketball practice, a special prep for the big game tomorrow. An agent had contacted him and told him scouts would be present, so he should bring his best game.

Nick always did, but tomorrow he needed to give 110%.

He changed and hit the court a bit before everyone else. A few other players tossed the ball around and shot easy baskets, but Nick grabbed a ball rack and went straight to the free-throw line. In his junior year, more than one scout mentioned his free throw percentage, so he'd practiced nearly every day over the summer and this entire season so far.

Every practice he started his warmups with foul shots, not stopping until he made at least ten in a row, and even when he reached the required number, he kept going until he missed. His record was thirty-three, and his free throw percentage had risen an impressive ten percent this year.

He missed the first shot. Not enough arc, his toss was much too flat, a common problem for guys his height and taller.

The second clanged off the back of the rim, bouncing away.

Relax, Nick, he told himself. His next attempt he took three breaths in and out, steadied his aim, and shot. Perfect swish. One.

Two. Three. Four. Five. Six. Seven, miss. So he started over. One. Two.

By the time he got to seventeen, the coach tapped him on the shoulder. "Great job, Nick, but today is a light scrimmage day."

Of course it was. The team followed the same routine every time before game day. He pushed the ball rack off the court and jogged up and down while the junior varsity came out on the floor.

"Start at center," his coach told him.

Nick cleared his mind. The only thing that mattered right now was the ball, the hoop, and his teammates. Life existed inside this court, and nowhere else.

He won the tip, hitting the ball to the team's point guard Tony, arguably the quickest guy on the team, and took off down the court. His teammate dribbled up, fast, and the JV fell back, leaving Nick open on the left side of the court, a fatal mistake since he was left-handed.

He put his hand high, and Tony nodded. As Nick moved toward the basket, Tony tossed the ball high and slow. Nick caught it one-handed, spun 180 degrees, and stuffed it home.

"Nice!" the coach shouted, clapping.

Nick ran back on defense, angling for the center of the zone, and picking up his man, the junior varsity center. Nick had to admit if he didn't hold the starting position, this kid would already be on the varsity, and once Nick graduated, he would be the heir apparent.

Not as tall as Nick, he was quicker on his feet. He came in fast, and turned around, posting up. Nick backed up, giving his opponent just a little space.

What the young center had yet to learn was the mental part of the game. A guard passed him the ball, and rather than passing it back out when Nick pressed him, he dribbled once and spun, trying a quick head fake.

Nick didn't fall for it but followed his opponent as he tried to fade away. He went up for the jumper, and Nick blocked the shot, knocking the ball out to one of his teammates, who led a fast break down the court. They scored again.

He felt limber. Refreshed even.

Whatever the game tomorrow would bring, Nick was ready.

2

DATE NIGHT

Nick stayed in the shower a bit longer than he needed to, but he wanted to be fresh for his date with Susie.

He liked her, and she him. He had no idea if their paths after college would continue to merge, or if they would go their separate ways, but for now, he was comfortable not knowing. The NBA was his dream, but it might not be hers, and although they talked about the future recently, they were still both playing it by ear.

She seemed equally happy to see where things might go. He thought of her smiling face as he shut off the water, dried himself, and got dressed.

He grabbed his bag and his camera from the locker room. He had an older Olympus with several lenses, and he liked almost everything about it. As any photographer he'd ever met, he wanted something new, better, but this camera had served him well through his minor and the photography classes that came with it. Many of the other students had much older equipment, so he couldn't complain.

His plan tonight was to take Susie to a small French restaurant downtown, one of her favorites, and then take her for a walk along the Freedom Trail. He planned to take several photos of her as they walked. Although portraits were not his specialty, he still got more than passable results, and she loved it when he photographed her.

An hour later, he pulled up in front of the apartment complex where she lived with a few friends. Nick had his own studio and again felt fortunate that his parents helped him with housing while he pursued his degree.

She bounded out dressed in a formal dress, but not one that was too long, even though it was chilly outside. She wore some kind of tights with it though, both because they were cute, and he imagined to keep her warm too.

He got out and went around to open the door for her. Susie was nearly a foot shorter than he was, and she stretched up on her tiptoes to give him a kiss. Her long blonde hair was tied up off her shoulders, and her emerald eyes sparkled. "I would have come up to get you."

"Nonsense," she said. "I couldn't wait. I'm starving."

"Well, our reservation awaits." Nick shut her door, raced around the front of the car, and slid into the driver's seat.

He looked over to see her holding his camera bag.

"Do you plan to photograph me this evening, Mr. O'Flannigan?"

"I do."

She clapped her hands. "Oh, good! I love that. Where are we going by the way?"

"French," he told her. "Followed by the Freedom Trail."

"Really?" She leaned over and kissed him again, this time for longer and with more meaning.

Behind them, a horn honked.

"Alright, alright." Nick waved at the person through his back window, although they probably couldn't see through the fogged glass.

Susie put her hand on his thigh as they drove downtown toward the restaurant. Nick placed his hand over hers when he could.

Typically, finding parking in Boston was near impossible, but he found a spot not far from both of their destinations.

The meal was delightful. They started with an appetizer, a bottle of wine too expensive for Nick, but one he splurged on anyway. The escargot was followed by foie gras, and then an entree he couldn't manage to pronounce. Everything was served on white linen tablecloths topped by candles.

Too full for dessert, he paid the bill and they wandered into the night. They began their walk near the car, proceeding from there. As they neared the North Church, he had Susie pose, capturing her perfectly silhouetted against the red brick.

She took his arm, staying close to fight the chill of the evening.

"So, graduation isn't far away," she started.

"Yes," Nick said. "Just around the corner really. Another five months, and we'll have to decide what to do with our lives."

He added a smile but could tell Susie was thinking about it, seriously.

"What do you think of your pro ball prospects, really?"

"Well, I have an agent looking out for me. Some scouts will be at the game tomorrow night, and he says if I look good, I have a reasonable shot to be a high pick in the draft."

"I know you have been working on things they were looking at. How is that going?"

"Good," he answered, thinking of practice that afternoon.

"And if you aren't drafted?"

They neared a narrow street and were for the moment sheltered from any wind. A metal lamppost beside the cobblestone streets intrigued him.

Gently taking Susie by the shoulders, he posed her next to the post and took a few shots.

"Smile," he told her.

She did, half-heartedly. When he lowered the camera, she moved back to him. "So if you don't get in?"

"Well, I'll still have my accounting degree."

She turned her face away, and Nick was unsure what troubled her. He thought everything was going well.

He looked at the last photo on the tiny screen. A frown danced at the corner of her eyes and mouth.

"Are you okay?" he asked. Snow started to fall, small, dry flakes that likely wouldn't stick unless the temperature dropped a little and they got thicker and wetter.

"Sure," she said. "I just worry about us, and what's next."

He took her hand, leading her back through what looked like a snow globe of old Boston and back toward his car.

"Don't worry about it," he told her. "We'll figure it out. We always do."

They fell into a comfortable silence. When they reached the car, they chatted about little things like study and the coming game the next day.

When he got to her place, she kissed him briefly on the mouth, tousled his thick, red hair with her tiny hand, and then opened her own door.

"See you tomorrow, Nick."

"Until then," he said. "I love you."

But her door closed, and she walked slowly into the dark. He watched her all the way to her apartment until she made it inside. Then he drove away.

Sleep came hard, and when he did close his eyes, he dreamed of dunking the ball in front of a huge crowd. He turned to look for Susie in the stands, but she wasn't there.

3

TAKING THE STAGE

Game day was vital to Nick. He didn't know if the French food the night before had been a mistake on his part because his stomach growled and rolled as he got out of bed. He headed to the kitchen for coffee and breakfast, hoping both would help.

Many college students got coffee on campus. Not Nick. He had his own stash at home and often cooked his own breakfast as well. He set up the coffee maker, quickly threw together an omelet, wolfed it down and grabbed his backpack, laptop, and camera.

He found he rarely went anywhere without it anymore. Every time he did, he regretted it, missing a shot here or a shot there, some photo-op he would try to capture with his phone, a poor substitute that seldom gave him the results he wanted.

He only had a couple of classes today, which he was happy for. As he headed out the door his phone rang.

"Hi, mom."

"Hi, Nick." His mom's delicate yet high-pitched voice revealed a deep Boston accent.

"Hey!" his father bellowed from the background. He seldom got on the phone anymore but relayed everything through Nick's mom at unbearable volume. He'd been going deaf for a while, but it had only gotten worse during Nick's time in college.

"Hey," Nick said. "How are you all doing?"

"Good," they replied in unison.

"You ready for the big game?" his dad yelled.

"Yes," he said. "All set." As he finished the sentence, a sense of dread came over him. His just finished breakfast sat heavy in his stomach. It growled unhappily.

Damn, he thought.

"We're planning to be at the game tonight. We know it's supposed to snow, but your father says he can drive in it just fine."

"I'm sure he can, Mom."

"Will those scouts be there tonight?"

"Yeah. My agent says they will."

"You're going to be a star, Nick."

"I--there are no guarantees." He wondered why he said it. The NBA was the dream he wanted more than anything. Without thinking, he reached out and rapped his knuckles on the table by the door.

Knock on wood.

"I believe in you," she said.

"We believe in you!" his father yelled. "You get them tonight. Show them what you're made of!"

Nick blinked a couple of times. He wasn't one to cry, not at simple things like that, but he was touched.

Then he set his jaw. His parents would be there tonight, and so would the scouts. Susie would be cheering him on. Everyone was rooting for his success.

So he would give them what they came for. He was good and knew he was. He'd been working hard, practicing, and he was ready.

Upset stomach or not, he would play the game of his life.

"I gotta go," he said, feeling his stomach do a slow forward roll. "I have a couple of classes before the game."

"Okay, son. See you tonight."

The call ended and he ran for the small bathroom in his apartment.

By noon, when his second class ended, Nick felt better. Sprite, lots of water, and a dose of stomach medicine helped.

But the rest of his body seemed to be carrying the weight of something, and it took him a bit to realize what it was: worry.

Nick never worried.

Maybe the walk would calm him.

He locked his backpack in a locker and went outside. He walked aimlessly around campus. He stopped frequently, taking photos of leaves dangling by web-like threads to tree limbs, naked branches reaching for the sky, and brown bushes dotting the snow-covered common areas. He focused on the little things that caught his eye, adding them to his already rich pre-game photography collection.

He might actually do something with it eventually. Everyone seemed to like them a lot.

Then the snow started, gently at first, but getting more intense.

Once inside, he headed for the common area of the student union building. He bought a salad, added some crackers to help his healing stomach, and sat down. A second later, Susie slid into the booth across from him.

"Hey," she said. "You ready for tonight?"

It was a big game. Everyone had to ask, but Nick had an oddly dark feeling every time they did.

"Just about. A light lunch and a quick stretching session, and I will be ready."

"You're going to do great." She put her hand on his forearm, and Nick took her hand in his.

"I know, but I can't help but be a little nervous."

"It's a big stage," she said. "But just a step away from a larger one."

Nick smiled at that. No pressure. Do well tonight, and the draft was only a couple of months away. But his agent told him he would know what teams, if any, were interested in him long before that.

"I know I will," he said, new confidence in his voice. "It's a game, just like any other one, right?"

Susie smiled. "I have to get ready, too. I just wanted to stop by and wish you luck. I'll be cheering from the sidelines."

She left Nick alone at the table after giving him a quick kiss on the cheek.

He finished his salad and headed for the locker room. He had to let go of the worry and clear his head for the game tonight.

But it was harder to shake than he thought it would be.

4

GAME ON

Nick ran out of the locker room and onto the floor. The arena was already filling in, and he spotted his parents and waved. He jogged up and down the court a couple of times and tossed in a few easy shots on their end of the court. The Georgia Tech players took the other end, and Nick stretched while looking their way.

Their big center concerned him. He was Nick's height, but broader shouldered. They'd played before, so Nick knew he wasn't as quick as he was, but he had long arms and a decent turnaround jump shot.

Tonight's game would be a mental one, with scouts here checking out all of the players. Nick secretly hoped a western team, maybe the Sonics, would pick him up before the Celtics had a chance to. It would be good to be somewhere else, not here, after college. Somewhere he and Susie could make a fresh start.

Just then he spotted her running in, her cheerleader uniform flattering her form, and her smile lighting his world. She waved and turned around as the cheerleaders started working the crowd too.

He looked over her head and saw his parents sitting in the third row. His dad waved and whistled loudly, and Nick waved back.

It was good to have them here.

The coach called them over to the bench, and Nick joined his teammates. The rest of the world would disappear for the next 90 minutes or so. The only thing his brain had room for was this court and whatever happened here.

Nick started and walked out for the tip-off.

He won, and hit the ball to his point guard, sprinted down the court, and outpaced the larger man guarding him. The ball soared, and Nick caught it mid-air, stuffing it in the basket in one smooth motion. 2-0.

Running back on defense he picked up his man, who turned around and posted up on him, pushing his hips into Nick, knocking him off balance, and holding his hand out for the ball.

He caught the pass, and Nick waited patiently, watching his body language as he dribbled once, twice.

He stopped, pivoted, and turned. He went up like he was going to take the shot, and Nick jumped with him, but at the last minute, his opponent dropped a pass to his incoming teammate who scored an easy layup.

Tied right off the bat.

Nick ran down the court again, this time matched stride for stride. He caught a bounce pass, dribbled, and passed back out to his left guard at the three-point line. A quick jumper put Boston College up by three.

The game went back and forth, each team scoring with few misses. Nick blocked one shot, tipped it to Boston's small forward, who threw it down the court for another score.

Boston 48, Georgia Tech 44.

The ball came back down, and Nick guarded the center loosely, giving him some room. Their guard threw a careless cross-court pass and Nick intercepted it. He ran the length of the court, passing the ball off to the teammate running with him.

He cut under the basket.

The ball soared and Nick went up to meet it, catching it and going for the dunk. A giant arm wrapped around his and pulled his shooting hand down. Nick stumbled and kept his feet, but just barely.

The whistle blew. Foul. Two free shots.

Georgia's center grinned at him.

Nick smiled back and walked to the foul line. His first shot swished right into the net. The second bounced twice on the rim and dropped through.

50-44. Halftime.

Nick had scored twelve of those points, not bad for a center, and two of them had been from the free-throw line.

He would've loved to know who the scouts were, but he didn't even look at the crowd. The most important thing was that his team won and that he kept performing well.

They headed for the locker room, but as they did the Georgia center caught his eye. He motioned with his fingers, pointing first to himself and then to Nick. Nick glared back.

His red hair came with the accompanying temper, and this guy's arrogance made him mad.

He put his fingers up in a "V", and pointed at his eyes, and then pointed a finger at his opponent. "I'm watching you," it meant.

A new calm settled over Nick, one he was intimately familiar with. He was in the zone. There was no stopping him now.

5

THE BIGGER THEY ARE

The second half tip went Nick's way again, and Boston scored right away. Georgia's first trip down the court, Nick stole the ball, running the court on another fast break. Score.

Up by eight.

The Georgia guard dribbled down, and the center posted up again. Nick let him, keeping his distance and his balance at the same time.

His opponent spun with a fadeaway jumper and threw the ball in over Nick's outstretched hand.

He grinned, but Nick shrugged it off.

He ran the court again, got the ball, threw it back outside, and another three rained down.

The back and forth kept going. Sometimes they scored, but Georgia kept pace with them shot for shot.

He was in the zone though. Every time Nick touched the ball, he made his shot. He had been four of five in the first half. This half he was perfect.

He drove inside on the next drive, got double-teamed, and fouled. He hit the first free throw and missed the second.

Two of three. Not the best, but he hadn't taken that many foul shots.

He'd have to correct that, get them to foul him more, so he could show his improvement. The next time Nick drove down the court, he dribbled inside, hard, and jumped for the basket as high and fast as he could.

Something solid, or rather someone, hit him across the shins, and he flipped through the air, sideways like a cartwheel. The world spun, his head traded places with his feet, and rushed past vertical.

The floor came up fast and his leg struck something, something unyielding.

Pain shot from his shin up through his hip and his entire right side.

He heard a scream, one that wasn't his, and he hit the floor with a loud thud. He blacked out.

When he came to, he was on his back. There were two members of the medical staff hovering over him.

"Don't move," one told him. "An ambulance is on the way."

There wasn't much chance of him moving, that was for sure. He didn't know what was wrong, or why he would need an ambulance, but he did know there was pain all along his right side, originating below his knee.

He was still on the court. The game stopped. He turned his head and saw several players from both teams kneeling in a circle not far away. They were praying for him. Not a good sign.

"How bad is it?" He asked.

"It's--we'll know more when we get you to the hospital. Just hang in there, Nick."

The next forty minutes or so were a blur. The ambulance came, and they moved him onto a stretcher. It hurt, but he grimaced through the pain. Susie followed them outside.

His parents were there, his mother pale and crying into his father's chest. His dad looked like he'd seen a ghost.

That was when he understood how bad it might be.

"It's broke, isn't it?"

One of the paramedics nodded. "Probably. Just hold still."

"Can I ride with him?" Susie asked.

The second paramedic looked at the first. "Sure, climb in."

"We'll meet you at the hospital!" his dad yelled.

The doors closed, and perhaps the bumpiest ride of Nick's life started.

They entered the ER, one paramedic pushing the stretcher, the other by his head. Nick wanted to close his eyes, to pass out from the pain, but he couldn't. He was on the border of too painful to function, not painful enough to lose consciousness.

It sucked.

The fluorescent rectangles rushed through his vision, and he felt himself turn as they pushed him into a cold room.

"Can't I go in with him?" he heard Susie ask.

"Not until we're done with the x-rays," a male voice told her. "He'll be right out."

"Is this--will I be okay?" Nick asked weakly.

"You'll be fine. This may be a bit painful, but I will try to take it as easy on you as possible," the male voice said. A masked face appeared over him. "It looks like this could have been much worse."

Nick closed his eyes, wishing for sleep, for rest, but it did not come. Someone draped a heavy blanket over him, and he heard the whir and click of an x-ray machine.

Lifted again, he felt a tug on his leg, and the pain shot up his entire right side with a fresh flame.

He heard a scream, distant, and realized it must have been him.

Whir, click.

"That should do it for now," the tech said.

The paramedics returned and wheeled him back into the hallway. Susie was there.

"I'll be with you every step of the way," she told him.

He was wheeled into a room, and he heard a thump as someone engaged the brakes on the rolling bed.

'We're going to transfer you now," someone said. He closed his eyes against the pain he knew would come.

Supported somehow, he felt himself lifted and then placed on a softer mattress. He groaned.

"I'm here," he heard Susie again.

"Mom and dad?" he asked.

"In the waiting area," she told him. "You'll be okay, Nick."

"Thank you." He could only manage two words, then closed his eyes again. The pain was unbearable.

Another female voice entered the room, and the new arrival and Susie shared a murmured conversation.

"You're going to feel a stick," he heard a moment later, "Then we will give you something to help you sleep."

He didn't feel a poke at all. But a moment later, he felt like he was drifting away, floating through a light-filled tunnel of some sort.

And then the darkness came.

6

THE END OF A DREAM

"We'll be done soon," the surgeon told his mom. "The surgery itself will take under an hour, but he'll be groggy for a bit. We'll send him home with some pain meds."

"He lives alone, in an apartment," he heard Susie say.

"He can stay with us!" His dad's yelled declaration made his head hurt, and he hoped Susie would jump in and rescue him somehow.

"I can stay with him at his place," Susie said.

"Maybe that would be best," he heard his mom say. "But I'm coming over every day to check on him and help where I can."

"I'm sure he would love that."

"I'll come, too!" his dad shouted.

'Oh, good," Susie said. "The more the merrier."

Nick thought she might be regretting her decision about now, but he was thankful. His parents' concern would taper off over time, and he had no desire to be in their house and underfoot for any length of time. It would be more stressful for him and for them.

"Thanks, Susie," he said. "And you too, mom and dad. I think I would be more comfortable in my own place, though."

He looked over and saw his mom smile at him. She'd probably made the offer out of kindness, not true desire. Nick loved his parents but moving out had been best for both him and them.

"I will be fine, don't worry."

"There's coffee in the waiting room," a male nurse told them. "And the Wi-Fi is decent if you need it."

He showed them out and Nick waved. Susie turned back to him and mouthed, "I love you."

Then the door closed.

"I want you to count backward from 100," the scrub-clad nurse by his head said.

"Okay." Nick started counting. "100, 99, 98, 97--"

He woke up what felt like a moment later, but hours must have passed. He could not move his leg and when he looked, found it was suspended in a sling about a foot over the bed. A plaster cast covered it from the thigh down, and there were a few metal attachments on the side.

"You're awake," he heard from beside him. "I'll get the surgeon for you."

A whirring started, and the head of the bed moved upward. He felt weak and tired, but the pain had dulled to a mild ache, at least for the moment.

A young man sporting a thin mustache that underlined a large nose framed by piercing green eyes entered the room. A stethoscope hung around his neck.

"Well, look who joined us."

"Yes," Nick said. "I seem to have made it."

"Indeed. You will be okay, and I am pretty sure if everything goes well this will be the only surgery you have to have."

"How bad?" Nick asked.

"You had a spiral fracture. We were able to twist things and put them back together, but you have some hardware in your leg. That will come out, eventually, but you'll always know the weather."

"Basketball?" He already suspected the answer.

"Not this year," the doc answered, shaking his head. "Maybe not ever. And you'll never be able to jump off your strong foot like you used to. I'm sorry man."

"Me, too," Nick struggled to not show his true emotion, but tears welled up behind his eyes.

"I watched you play," the doctor told him. "You had a real shot. You can try rehab, but it would be a challenge to get back to where you were before."

"How long will I be in the cast?"

"Six to eight weeks. We'll take the pins out in about four or five, once we check things out with x-rays. You'll probably be walking again in about five months or so."

"Five months?"

"Listen, take it easy, and you'll fully recover. Try to rush things? Well, I can't tell you what will happen."

Nick just nodded.

"You up to seeing your family? I think your dad may pass out if he can't see you soon."

"Sure, send them in," Nick said.

The doctor left, and a few minutes later the door opened slowly. Susie entered the room, followed by his parents.

"How's my boy?" his mom asked.

"I'm okay," he answered, watching Susie's eyes as she looked down at the cast, the hardware.

"They tell us you can go home tomorrow?" his dad said, his voice only a few decibels above a normal tone.

"Yeah," Nick answered. "Crutches for a while for sure."

"That's good," his mom responded. "We can get you some real food. I can't believe what they try to serve you in here."

Nick smiled. "That would be good." He didn't feel hungry. Not yet. His mind was numb. In 48 hours he'd gone from NBA candidate to a cripple.

He didn't want to think about it too much.

"Will you be able to play again?" Susie asked the question no one else dared to.

Nick shook his head. "Probably not."

He saw her tears as she looked away.

"A few of the guys from your team and your coach are here to see you," his mom told him.

Nick just nodded. He would have to face that reality sooner or later. It might as well be now.

"We'll let you be," his parents said. "We'll be here tomorrow to help get you home."

They left. Susie stayed. Four of the players on the team and his coach came in a few minutes later. They joked around, laughed, and the coach took a moment to pray for him. Then they too, left. He and Susie were alone.

And he knew then that his life had changed forever. He was no longer a member of the team. His plans were over. He would have to fall back onto plan B.

Accounting.

And that without the buffer of an NBA career.

Susie held his hand in silence, clearly sensing what they both needed.

Overwhelmed with grief, Nick concentrated on taking one breath at a time, the warmth of her hand in his.

He drifted off into sleep.

When he woke, Susie was gone, the room was empty, and he was alone.

7

PICTURE THE FUTURE

Eight Weeks Later

"You'll be fine," the therapist said. He unstrapped Nick from the motion machine, one that had been moving his leg for him, stretching it further each visit. Next week, he would start his weight training.

He struggled to his feet and reached for his crutches.

"How long will I need these?"

"Eh, another couple of weeks. You'll be walking in no time now that you are out of your cast and the pins have been removed."

"How long will I limp?"

"That depends on you. You'll walk normally again, more than likely, but you will have a limp if you push too hard."

"Great. I'm 23, and I'm an old man."

"Don't be discouraged. It could have been much worse. Your surgeon was fantastic. He did an amazing job."

"No more basketball though."

"You can play in rec leagues from time to time if you feel up to it. But be careful. And you probably won't win any MVP awards. Running will be tough. Jumping? Well, with your height, you might still be able to dunk, but not easily. Landing will hurt."

"Thanks. I'll live with it I suppose."

"You'll get used to it."

Nick shook the man's hand, went to the front desk, and arranged his next appointment. Then he walked out into the sunlight. He put his sunglasses on and headed for his car, swinging between his crutches pretty effortlessly.

At least my upper body is getting a workout, he thought.

As he reached the driver's door, he looked over and saw there was a stone pillar in a flower garden in the center of the parking lot. A yellow flower grew behind it, and it would make a great photo. He unlocked the car, opened the back door instead, and removed his camera, the Olympus he'd had all through college, and slung it around his neck. Carefully, he crutched over the pavement toward the flower garden. He studied the shot, raised his camera, and framed the flower.

Not quite right. It would be better if he could get lower. *Lower?* he thought. *On crutches?*

Then he looked again. "I can do this," he said out loud.

He set his left crutch against one of the stones surrounding the flower garden, and then lowered himself using the right one for support, keeping his leg as straight as he could, taking all his weight on his left foot. When he got low enough, he also put his left hand down and lowered himself to the ground. The pavement was warm, but not overly so.

He raised his camera again, framed the flower and the pillar, and took the shot. Perfect. He took a few more just to be sure, and then looked at his current position. His right leg stuck straight out front, his left one was bent, and he was leaning back on one hand, shooting photos with the other. He laughed.

"Oh my God!" he heard from behind him. He heard footsteps pounding and turned his head.

The physical therapist was rushing toward him, another staff member right behind.

"Are you okay?" the man asked, out of breath. Then he stopped.

Nick smiled and pointed at the camera. "Yeah, I just got down here to get a photo."

"A what?"

Nick awkwardly pushed himself forward, and held out the camera, screen toward the therapist. "Check it out."

"Are you crazy? I thought you fell."

"Nope," Nick said. "I did this on purpose. Although I didn't think through getting back up as clearly as I probably should have."

"Really? Do you think so?" the therapist scoffed.

Nick grinned, and the other staff member stared at him too. "Let's get him up," she said.

They helped Nick to his feet, and he thanked them. Both the therapist and his co-worker walked on either side of him until he got into his car.

He waved, and then pulled out of the parking lot.

When he arrived home, he saw both Susie's car and his parents' SUV parked at the curb. He wondered what they were doing.

He awkwardly got out of the car, grabbed his camera bag from the back seat, and replaced his camera inside. He couldn't wait to share the photo on social media. He'd developed quite a following with some great macro shots he'd taken lately around the house and on his frequent visits to specialists and doctors.

Little details seemed to be his favorite, and he loved macro photography. It soothed him even when he was stressed about school.

And he was almost done. One more final and he would have his Bachelor's in Accounting with a minor in photography.

His plan B had become his plan A.

Susie burst out of the front door and ran to him. She took his camera bag and kissed him on the cheek. "What happened? You're all dirty. Did you fall?"

"No," he said. "I got down on the ground to get a photo of a flower I saw."

"Are you sure that was a good idea?"

"My therapist didn't think so when he ran out to pick me up."

"Oh, Nick."

"Are mom and dad here? What is going on?"

"Well, they got you an early graduation present. And given the circumstances, I think it is oddly appropriate."

"Okay," Nick said nervously.

"C'mon," she said. There were three short steps to get into the house, and Nick navigated them like a pro. His parents sat in the living room sharing his small couch. He hoped to move soon. This place had been fine when he was in college, but he was ready for a larger, more adult apartment.

There were a few cheap lamps around the room, none of them currently on. A large, well-used recliner sat in one corner, the place Nick had to sleep for the first little while after the surgery. Nick moved to it and sat down heavily, leaning his crutches against the tall side table beside it.

A low coffee table sat in the center of the room, and on it were two packages, one long, thin one and one large, rectangular one.

"What's this?" he asked.

"Well, Nick," his mom started. "We know this has been hard for you, and we are so proud that you are graduating."

"I haven't graduated yet."

"You will soon."

"If I pass," Nick joked. His GPA was stellar, even with how rough this semester had been.

"Nick, stop," Susie said. She put her hand on his arm, and Nick shut his mouth. This was an important moment for his parents. He shouldn't ruin it with jokes.

"We want you to have this!" his father nearly shouted. "Open it."

"Nick, yes," his mother emphasized. "Your father is so excited." She put her hand on his dad's knee.

He sighed and grabbed the long, thin package first. "This one okay?"

"Sure," his mom said, exchanging a sly look with his dad.

Nick tore open a corner of the paper, and then ripped the rest off, revealing a Manfroto tripod, a top-of-the-line model.

"Wow," he said. "This is amazing!"

"Yes, yes," his mom said before he could open the box. "Open the next one."

Nick grabbed the next package and opened a corner. He peeked at the box, and then ripped some more.

It was an Olympus camera. A brand new one, the latest EMIX model.

"No way," he said. "This is amazing!"

He opened the box and felt the new camera with his hand. He removed it from the foam packaging.

"Mom, Dad, I can't thank you enough," he said.

"You are so welcome," his mom said.

They watched as he unpackaged it and plugged the provided battery into the slot. It showed only a 25% charge, but that would do for what Nick wanted.

"Susie, can you unbox the tripod?" he asked.

"Sure," she said. Nick fiddled with the camera while she removed the tripod from the box and wrapper. Nick took the camera mount from her.

"Can you set it up right here?" He gestured to a spot on the floor close to him.

"What are you doing?" his mom asked.

"Taking my first photo with my new camera," he said.

8

A NEW DREAM

Nick adjusted the camera settings and put it on the tripod.

"Susie, over there please," he said.

He issued instructions to her and his parents, adjusted the light, and snapped a few test shots.

"Now, everyone smile," he said.

"Cheese!" his dad shouted.

Everyone laughed, and Nick caught the moment. Susie moved out of the frame, insisting that he take some shots with just his parents in them. He did, some of the best photos he'd ever seen of the two of them.

"Now you get in there," Susie said.

Nick obeyed, setting his crutches to the side so they would not be in the photo. She took a few shots of the three of them without moving the camera or changing the settings.

When they were done, his parents excused themselves.

"We have to go," his mom told him. "I need to get your father dinner and his medication."

"Sounds good," he said, feeling tired himself.

But there was one more thing he wanted to do tonight.

"You want me to go, too?" Susie asked.

"No. I was thinking of ordering in."

"That would be nice," she said, sliding her hand up his arm. "What did you have in mind?"

"Your favorite, that Chinese place."

"Sounds great." She kissed him on the cheek.

Nick called and placed the order, and then went to his room to change. He did so, with some difficulty, but into some comfortable sweats. Dressing was much easier without the cast on his leg. He slipped a small box into his pocket.

A knock sounded on the door a few minutes later, and they collected their delivery. They ate in Nick's small dining room. He picked at his food, nervous. Susie picked up on it.

"Are you okay?" she asked.

"Of course," he said. "I just--you know I love you, right?"

"And I love you," she replied.

"Can you come to the living room? I want to talk to you."

"Sure." Susie moved to sit on the couch.

"No, no," he said. "Can you sit in my chair?"

The light outside was failing, and Nick turned on one of the lamps. He struggled to position the tripod and camera, focusing on Susie and the chair.

"What are you doing?" she asked. "Can I help?"

"I got this," Nick said. He was a little out of breath, and his leg did hurt, but nothing would ruin this moment.

"Okay." He could see by her frown and the lines on her forehead that she was worried.

"This thing has a long timer. Let's see if I can get into a picture with you," he said.

"Nick, I can push the button. I can move faster than you," she said.

"I got it," he answered.

Nick set the timer for thirty seconds, and then hobbled to her side, pulling the small box from his pocket as he went. She moved to stand, but Nick lowered himself to the ground, much like he had to get the photo this afternoon, only sitting more upright.

"Susie," he said.

She looked down at him, concern in her eyes. "Nick, what are you--"

"Will you marry me?" He quickly opened a tiny box and presented it to her.

Her eyes went wide as she saw what he held, and her hands flew to her mouth.

The shutter snapped, the camera flashed, and he'd captured it. The perfect moment.

"Of course, Nick!" she said. "A thousand times, yes!"

Nick smiled, and she hugged him, kissed him, and moved out of the way. "You need to sit here," she said. "You can't stay on the floor that way. You look ridiculous."

Nick found that he did need to sit. His legs hurt, his back and every muscle in his body seemed to be sore. But her "yes" had sent a wave of relief over him.

Susie helped him into the chair once she had slipped the ring onto her finger.

Nick let her and then asked her to bring him the camera. She did.

She sat on his lap, carefully on his left leg, and they looked through the photos he had taken that evening.

"You know, Nick, you are really good at this. That macro shot you took earlier today was amazing, and I am glad you captured our proposal. Look."

He looked at the photo. He had to admit, it was good. Better than he thought he was capable of.

"You should think about taking photos and selling them on the side."

"Really?"

"Yeah, set up a website, an online store. You could take photos for businesses and stuff too."

"You think so?"

"Your social media followers would love them. I bet they would buy them too."

"But I'm an accountant."

"Not yet. You still have to pass your tests. Besides, you can do both, at least for a while."

"You think so?"

"I do."

"Maybe I'll give it a shot."

"A shot?" she said. "Is that one of your dad's horrible puns, Nick?"

"Well, I guess you could say that," he replied.

"Come here, you." She kissed him, lightly at first, and then more deeply.

When they came up for air, she looked at him. "When are you telling your parents?"

"Tomorrow. You know mom will want to have a dinner or something."

"I know. That's good. But what should we do with the rest of our evening?"

"I--do you want to tell anyone?" Nick asked.

"Not tonight," she said. "I think someone needs to go to bed."

"Yeah," he agreed with a sigh.

"And you need to come with me," Susie said.

"Oh, yes, I mean, of course," he stammered.

"Follow me, you big stud."

Nick got his crutches and followed her into his room.

An hour later, she was asleep in his arms, snoring softly into his shoulder.

Nick lay awake though, thinking. Maybe he could take photos on the side. It might make a great business and offer him a lot of freedom.

And it was much less of a contact sport than basketball.

In the morning, he would see if he could set up a website. Maybe he could get a clever domain. One like macrophotography4u.com.

With that thought, he fell into a restful and deep sleep. He had odd dreams, one of taking photos of large, domed buildings, and at one point in the night, he dreamed of being stung by a bee while taking a photo. He woke with a start.

The room was dark. Susie slept in his arms. And all was right with the world. Tomorrow would be a new day, and he felt like it would be only the beginning of a great adventure.

Nick is now on the assignment of his life.

Fast forward from *Fast Break*, and you'll find Nick O'Flannigan traveling the country from state capital to state capital, photographing capitol buildings and finding murder in each city.

> "At a time when we can't travel, Nick's story is a great escape." B. Worley, Amazon Reader

If you loved this book, I would love it if you would leave a review. It's one of the things we as authors love most.

If you want to keep up with Nick and his adventures, subscribe to our newsletter . We'll only send you bargain books and let you know when new stories are coming. You'll never miss a release.

We also have audiobooks! Lots of them. Check those out on Audible, ACX, or wherever you purchase audio books. Our narrator, Joseph Stevenson and the team at Larson Sound Studios do a great job on them.

In the meantime, be well. Nick and I will see you as we travel the country together!

THE "CAPITAL CITY MURDERS"
SERIES

"Fast Break"

Book #1 "Overdoses in Olympia"*

Book #2 "Slaying in Salem"*

Book #3 "Strangled in Sacramento"*

Book #4 "deCapitated in Carson City"*

Book #5 "Buried in Boise"*

"The Wicked West"—a compilation of books 1-5, available in both e-books and print*

Book #6 "Hanging in Helena"*

Book #7 "Branded in Bismarck"*

Book #8 "Parricide in Pierre"*

Book #9 "Carnage in Cheyenne"*

Book #10 "Defenestration in Denver"*

"The Nick of Time"—a compilation of books 6-10, available in both e-books and print*

Book #11 "Silenced in Salt Lake"*

Book #12 "Poisoned in Phoenix"*

Book #13 "Stung in Santa Fe"*

Book #14, "Axed in Austin"*

Book #15: "Offered in Oklahoma"*

*These books are now available in audio format!

All the books in the "Capital City Murders" series are available at www.CapitalCityMurders.com and your favorite e-book seller.

FROM OVERDOSES IN OLYMPIA

Another Overdose

Mary slipped her arms into the white sweater, the one with the name tag Mary Lawson, RN attached. She took one final sip of her coffee, poured out the rest, and paused. *What did I miss? The patient had come in with a shattered right leg and an arm broken in two places. Thank God he was wearing a helmet, or he might have been taken to the morgue instead of to the hospital. He seemed healthy other than the injuries from the motorcycle accident.*

She'd been racking her brain for the past two days trying to figure out what happened, why the accident victim overdosed. He was under her care, and she did everything that any nurse would do in the same situation. The odd part was, the patient had been almost ready to go home.

Sure, he seemed a bit melancholy, but who wouldn't be after that kind of accident? It seemed odd.

There would be an autopsy, of course, and that would show exactly what caused his death. That would take at least two weeks.

Mary looked at her watch. She should be heading to work. The drive to Mercy Hospital took her past the location on the freeway where the motorcycle had been sideswiped, and she grimaced as she passed the spot. There was a piece of shiny metal on the right shoulder she hadn't seen before. Was it from the accident?

"Good morning, Mary," the guard said as Mary pulled into the employees' secure parking area and lowered her window.

"Good morning, John," she replied. "How's it going?"

"Pretty quiet so far," he answered as he pushed the button to raise the gate. "Have a good day."

"You, too." Mary raised her window and drove to her favorite parking spot. Close to an entrance, it was shaded in the afternoon. She disliked getting into a hot car, but even worse she hated leaving the windows down and having the elm leaves blow inside. There was something in those leaves that set off her allergies and made her sneeze uncontrollably.

Once inside, Mary put her purse in her locker and took the staff elevator to the fourth floor.

"Good morning, Pat," Mary said as she approached the nurses' area.

Pat looked up from her paperwork. "Hi, Mary. You know I am always glad to see you, and not just because you're taking over."

"I know. I see a new name on the board. What's he in for?"

"Mainly observation," the departing nurse said. "He works at a lumber mill and was hit in the head with more than just the proverbial two by four. A CT scan didn't show any abnormalities, but the ER doc wanted to hold him for twenty-four hours just to make sure. He will probably go home sometime during your shift, so you'll give him his instructions and meds to go home with."

"Well, let's go over the shift handoff report so you can go home and get some rest," Mary said as she pulled a chair.

Mary started her own rounds thirty minutes later. She entered room 414, the one with the new patient. The woman who'd been in there for the last few days had gone home last night. The room was now Robert's, and his alone at least for the next few hours. A putrid smell hit her as she stepped further inside.

Flatulence. The kitchen needs to stop serving so much beans and broccoli.

She cleared her throat as she stepped around the curtain to see her new patient, who completely filled the length of the standard hospital bed.

Robert looked up at her and smiled.

"Good morning, Robert. My name is Mary Lawson, and I'm the RN on duty, so you'll be seeing a lot of me today." She caught his eyes checking her out. Her face flushed slightly as she tried to maintain her composure.

She cleared her throat.

"How are you feeling? I see in your chart that you took quite a blow to the head." Mary glanced up from the screen that held his electronic patient chart.

Robert extended his right hand over his reclining body as Mary awkwardly reached across the space separating them and shook his hand. He could probably fit both her hands inside one of his. "Nice to meet you, Mrs. Lawson," he said in a deep voice.

"It's Miss Lawson, but that's okay. Actually, Mary is fine."

What was this awkward feeling coming over her?

Mary gently pulled her hand back. "Your hand seems a bit cool," she said as she looked at his vitals that had been taken just about an hour ago. "Are you in any pain right now?"

"I do have a headache, but the doc last night said I probably would for a few days. It's pretty normal considering. He also said I might be able to go home today?"

"That's up to him," Mary said and looked back at the chart. "You've had enough acetaminophen that it should've taken care of your pain, but I can get you something stronger if you'd like."

"Sure," he said. "That would be great. If the doc could send me home with something just in case, that would be good too."

"I'll get some prescription naproxen for you. Like Aleve, only a little stronger. Have you had that before?"

Robert shrugged. "I think so."

"Okay. I'll bring some in a bit and see if I can get you a bottle to go, so to speak. Need anything else at the moment?"

He just smiled and looked up at her through his arched bushy eyebrows. "No, ma'am. Thank you."

Mary felt warm. She unconsciously grabbed the front of her sweater and flapped it to try to cool herself down. "You're welcome, Robert, but you don't have to thank me. That's what we're here for, to help you get better. I should be back within a few moments with something for that pain." Mary turned and left the room. She sensed Robert's eyes following her until the curtain blocked his view.

A few minutes later, Mary made it back into room 414, carrying a small dispensing cup holding two capsules. "Knock, knock," she said as she entered the room. Some sports station was on the television. The same odor hit her as she stepped past the curtain. "Who's winning?"

"They are just replaying old games," Robert said as he used his bulging arms to push his body into a more upright position.

"Thank you," Robert said as he tossed the capsules to the back of his mouth and swallowed them without any water.

"If you drink something, it will help them get into your system faster."

"Yes, ma'am," he replied as he took the cup of water from the tray and emptied it in three huge gulps.

"I'll be back later to check on you. Maybe even to send you home. Need anything else?"

"No, ma'am," Robert said as he let his long, well-muscled body slide back down into the bed. Her eyes instinctively watched his movements as if in slow motion.

"I'll close the door, but you can always press your call button if you need anything." Mary pulled the door closed behind her. The cool air in the hall felt really good.

A few hours passed quickly, and around the time for her noon rounds, Mary got the discharge papers for room 414. She gathered up the prescription bottle of capsules the pharmacy had sent up. Pulling up the forms for him to sign on her tablet, she made her way to his room.

Since her hands were full, she knocked softly and went in. The room was now very quiet, and the odor that previously plagued the room was gone.

Robert was laying on his side, sleeping, and she woke him gently.

"Robert?"

He sat up, still seeming to be a bit groggy. Not a great sign for a guy who might have had a concussion. "I'm awake," he managed to say.

"Let me check a few things really quick," Mary said, a bit concerned.

She took out her penlight and shined it in each eye. Pupils were reactive. She felt the pulse on his neck, and it felt strong and normal.

"You seem to be okay. I'm going to have you sign these discharge papers. We do it on these tablets now, and then I can print it out for you. But I am going to have the doctor check you out before you leave."

Robert smiled, seeming to be coming back from his impromptu nap. "Sounds good. I guess those pills really did help with the headache."

"Here are your ones to take home," she told him. "No more than one every twelve hours. You can get dressed now, and I will be right back."

Mary walked down the hall to the nurses' station, hitting the print button as she went.

She grabbed Robert's paperwork as it spat out of the printer. Reaching for the phone to page the doctor on call, she saw the call light came on above his door and heard the chime at the desk.

Without hesitating, Mary sprinted down the hall back to the room. She heard a crash as she opened the door.

Robert was on the floor, face red as if he was choking. Lying beside him on the floor was an open pill bottle.

For a moment, she caught a whiff of almonds.

Mary knelt beside him and felt his neck for a pulse. There wasn't one.

She dropped his arm and pressed the call button again, yelling into the speaker: "Crash cart! Stat. Four fourteen. Now!"

Immediately she started CPR. Help seemed to take an eternity to arrive, even though she knew it was only seconds. Her arms already felt heavy as she continued compressions on his chest.

A doctor arrived followed closely by another nurse pushing a cart. Mary moved aside as the doctor put his stethoscope to the man's hairy chest.

"Still no pulse," he said.

The other nurse turned on the fully charged defibrillator. "Ready," she said.

The doc grabbed the paddles and placed them on the patient's chest. "Clear," he said, and the nurse flipped the switch. Mary watched in haunted silence as Robert's body shook from the electric charge coursing through him. The doctor listened again for a heartbeat. There was none. He applied the paddles again. Another shock. Still nothing.

He threw the paddles aside and resumed CPR, pressing down hard on the chest and counting aloud, "One, two, three." Doc counted to ten and placed his ear near the patient's mouth. Still no breath. After several futile attempts, he stood back.

"He's gone, I'm sorry." The doc looked at the bottle and capsules on the table. "He must've overdosed."

"Why would he do that?" Mary said. "He was on his way out."

"I have no idea," the doctor said.

No! Mary's mind churned in anguish. *Not another overdose! And both of them had occurred when she was on duty.*

ABOUT THE AUTHOR

Troy Lambert is a full-time writer and author. Having written over two dozen mysteries and other novels, Troy is well-versed in story creation, and he knows what it takes to make a fictional story real! Troy's hobbies and pastimes (when he's able to break away from the computer) include hiking into the mountains of Southwest Idaho, fishing in a fast-rushing stream, and going for a drive where his mind can work on creating that perfect twist to the book he's currently writing. A native of Idaho Falls, Idaho, Troy and his wife live in Meridian, Idaho. You can find his other works, including his latest book, *Teaching Moments*, at troy-lambertwrites.com.

ALSO BY TROY LAMBERT

The Max Boucher Series:

Teaching Moments

Harvested

The Samuel Elijah Johnson Series

Redemption

Temptation

Confession

Monster Marshals

Miner Inconveniences

Tilting at Windmills

Non-Fiction

The Tao of Trek

Writing as a Business: Production, Distribution, and Marketing

7 Steps to Plotting Your Novel Quickly

The Dog Complex

Stray Ally